Sherlock Bones

and the Missing Cheese

by
Susan Stevens Crummel

illustrated by
Dorothy Donohue

AMAZON CHILDREN'S PUBLISHING

What's **that** smell **in the Dell?**

Do tell!

W - - e - - l - - l . . . . it comes from a cheese.
A great big cheese. A smelly, scrumptious cheese,
if you please. Made from the milk of a cantankerous
cow—oh, wow! The one-horned, two-eared,
three-legged Cowabunga. She likes to kick,
so you'd best be quick when you
milk **that** cow—and **how**!
   The folks in the Dell keep
that cheese on a huge gray stone,
all alone. Why? Because it's smelly.
Really smelly!

   But, my, is it scrumptious!

BIG CHEESE

So scrumptious that once a month, when the moon is full, everyone gathers around that cheese—that smelly Cowabunga cheese. They dance and they prance until midnight, when the time is right. Then they all take a bite!

"**Ahhhh!**"
they sigh.
"**Ohhhh!**"
they cry.
One little bite . . . sc**rumptious**!
And so it is and always was—
except for one fateful night, because . . .

"LOOK!"

"SEE!"

BIG

"It can't **be**!"
"The Cowabunga cheese is **gone**!"
There were cries and moans, wails and groans.
Then Farmer Jones yelled,

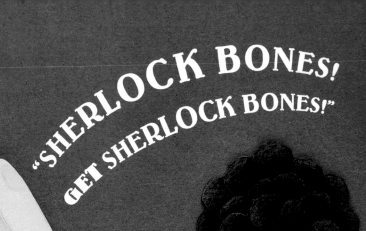

Sherlock Bones
can crack any case,
any kind, any place.
He can solve any
crime, anywhere,
any time.

How does he do it?

He **looks**.

He **listens**.

He **tastes**.

He **touches**.

He **smells**.

He uses his **senses**—
he's a sensible hound.

Then he opens his book, his little black book, and writes the clues down.

So on that night, that cheeseless night, Farmer Jones found Sherlock Bones.
"The Cowabunga cheese is gone!"
"Oh, no! Let's go! To the Dell—tallyho!"
said Sherlock.
Sherlock took his little black book,
jumped to the floor, and dashed out
the door.

The folks in the Dell
were all in a dither.
"Who would seize our
scrumptious cheese?"
"Quiet, please!" cried Sherlock Bones.
"Did anyone **see** anything last night?"
"I did," said the farmer's wife. "It was strange, very strange.
I saw the moon glow oh, so bright. Then all of a sudden—
no moon, no light!"

"H-m-m-m-m-m-m." Sherlock wrote a note in his book.

"Did anyone **hear** anything last night?"

"I did," said Cat. "It was strange, very strange. I heard a growl. A great big growl. Sounded like a bear, but I couldn't swear."

"H-m-m-m-m-m-m."

Sherlock wrote a note in his little black book.

"Did anyone **smell** anything last night?"

"I did," said Rat. "It was strange, very strange. I usually smell that great big cheese. Ahhhh, that cheese, that scrumptious cheese! But last night there was a different smell. Hard to tell, but I think that smell was . . . was . . . tomatoes!"

"H-m-m-m-m-m-m." Sherlock wrote a note in his book.

Then, with his nose to the ground, that brilliant hound started sniffing around. He picked up a scent, and off he went.

sniff! SNIFF!

Sherlock Bones
sniffed his way right up to the muffin shop.
"Hungry, Sherlock?" asked the Muffin Man. "Try my
new Huffin' Puffin' Cheesy Muffins. Fresh from the oven and made
with the most scrumptious cheese!"
Sherlock sniffed. "Ah, where did you get such a smelly, scrumptious cheese?"
"It was strange, very strange," said the Muffin Man. "I was outside feeding my
cat when—SPLAT!—slices of cheese landed right on my hat."

"H-m-m-m-m-m-m." Sherlock wrote a note in his book.

Then, with his nose to the ground, that brilliant hound started sniffing around. He picked up a scent and off he went.

sniff! SNIFF!

Sherlock Bones sniffed his way right up to the foot of the beanstalk.

MISTER MUFFIN

SMELLY!

LICK! LICK! LICK!

"scrumptious!"

"H-m-m-m-m-m-m-m, I think we have a giant problem!"

sniff! SNIFF!

Sherlock Bones sniffed his way right up, up, up the beanstalk to Giant's house.

"That place is gigantic!" He started to
panic and then became frantic. "I can't go
in there—it says STRANGERS BEWARE!"

STRANGERS
BEWARE

Then . . .
a stinky smell filled the air.
There was Giant, making
giant pizzas—and a giant mess!
He tossed the gooey dough,
stirred the bubbly tomato sauce,
and grated huge hunks of cheese wildly.

A slice hit Sherlock.

LICK! LICK! LICK!

"Yum, yum!"

"Fe, Fi, Fo, **FUM.**

**Who's that saying
'Yum, yum'?"**

"Sherlock Bones, brilliant bloodhound, and you, Sir, have stolen the big cheese."

"Yeah? So what? I was hungry. Gut-growlin' hungry. Hungry for pizza. I smelled cheese, and there it was—alone on the stone. I needed a meal. No big deal."

"It most certainly **is** a big deal, Sir!" barked Sherlock Bones. "That cheese is special. It's one of a kind—made from the milk of Cowabunga. It belongs to the folks who dwell in the Dell. It's not your snack—so give it back. Right **now!**"

"No! It's **mine**! I want it **all**!"
Giant stuffed every last bit of
cheese into his giant mouth. He
munched and he crunched, he
chomped and he chewed. Then,
in one giant gulp, he swallowed.

burp! BURP!
BUrRRRrp!

"I feel sick—it's that cheese!"
Giant held his stomach and fell
to his knees.

Then he
lost his balance
and started to yell.
"HELLLLP!"
He grabbed at Sherlock.

Together they fell . . .

down, down, down toward the Dell.

THUMP! burp! burp! THUMP!

"It's the Giant!" yelled Farmer Jones.
"He stole your cheese," cried Sherlock Bones.
"He ate it all before the fall!"

Giant moaned. "I don't feel right."

"That's why we eat just one small bite," scolded Nurse.

"Help me!" pleaded Giant.

Nurse wagged her finger. "You have Cowabunga cheese disease. I could help, but first say please."

"**Please!**"

"And you must promise to come here every day, milk Cowabunga, and make a new cheese."

"**I promise!**"

"And you must make sure the cheese is never stolen again."

"OK!" yelled Giant. "**I'll make sure!**"

Nurse smiled, "I'll get the cure!"

It was the night
of the next full
moon. Everyone
gathered around the cheese. The new, smelly
Cowabunga cheese. They danced and they pranced until
midnight, when the time was right. Then they all took a bite!

"Ahhhh!" they sighed.

"Ohhhh!" they cried.

One little bite . . . scrumptious!
Farmer Jones smiled with delight.
"Sherlock Bones, you're always right!"
"Yay for Sherlock!"
"Brilliant hound!"
"Top dog!"
"Best around!"
"Don't be cheesy. It was easy! You can do it,
if you choose! Pay attention. Look for clues.
Use your senses. You can't lose!"

← **Sherlock's Clues**

The story of *Sherlock Bones and the Missing Cheese* was inspired by the popular children's song "The Farmer in the Dell."

Well, not really . . .

For my sister Janet, who, like Sherlock, helps willingly and tirelessly —s.s.c.

**To my favorite Wisconsin Cheeseheads, Nancy, Mary, and Peg.
And my 2 little cheese curds, Julia and Joe. —D.D.**

Amazon Publishing
Attn: Amazon Children's Books
P.O. Box 400818
Las Vegas, NV 89149
www.amazon.com/amazonchildrenspublishing

Library of Congress Cataloging-in-Publication Data
Crummel, Susan Stevens.
Sherlock Bones and the missing cheese / by Susan Stevens Crummel ;
illustrated by Dorothy Donohue. — 1st ed.
    p. cm.
Summary: When the wonderful, smelly, scrumptious cheese made once a
month out of the milk of a one-horned, two-eared, three-legged cowabunga is
stolen from the dell, Sherlock Bones is enlisted to find out what happened.
ISBN 978-0-7614-6186-9 (hardcover)
ISBN 978-0-7614-6187-6 (ebook)
[1. Stories in rhyme. 2. Cheese—Fiction. 3. Dogs—Fiction. 4. Stealing—Fiction.
5. Characters in literature—Fiction.] I. Donohue, Dorothy, ill. II. Title.
PZ8.3.C88644Sh 2012
[E]—dc23
2011032178

The illustrations are rendered in
    layered cut paper with colored pencil.
Book design by Virginia Pope
Editor: Margery Cuyler

Printed in China (W)
First edition
10 9 8 7 6 5 4 3 2 1